MAI

Maresca offers something beyond the usual high fantasy fare, with a wealth of unique and well-rounded characters, a vivid setting, and complicatedly intertwined social issues that feel especially timely.

— PUBLISHERS WEEKLY

Marshall Ryan Maresca is one of the most ambitious fantasy authors to burst on the scene in the last decade.

— BLACK GATE MAGAZINE

I love the complexity of Marshall Ryan Maresca's worldbuilding as the vast conspiracy underlying all the inner workings of Maradaine is emerging through the intertwining pieces coming together. It's nothing short of brilliant!

— FRESH FICTION

It's a story about morality, about sacrifice, about what people want from life. It's a fun story—there's quips, swordfights, chases through the streets. It's a compelling, convincing work of fantasy, and a worthy addition to the rich tapestry that is the works of Maradaine.

— SCI-FI AND FANTASY REVIEWS

In one fast-paced, funny, highly readable novel after another, Maresca continues to build out every nook and alleyway of Maradaine, which is fast becoming one of the most richly detailed settings in fantasy.

— BARNES & NOBLE SCI-FI AND FANTASY BLOG

Definitely a fun read, and one classic fantasy fans will likely enjoy.

— BIBLIOTROPIC

HULTICHIA

ALSO BY MARSHALL RYAN MARESCA

From DAW Books

ALSO BY MARSHALL RYAN MARESCA

From Artemisia Books

The Mystical Murders of Yin Mara

Hultichia

The Withered Boy*

The Royal First Irregulars*

A Proper Lady of Society*

*-Forthcoming

HULTICHIA

A MARADAINE SAGA STORY

MARSHALL RYAN MARESCA

ARTEMISIA

Chronological Note

Hultichia takes place in the autumn of the year 1213 by the Druth calendar, two years before the events of *The Thorn of Dentonhill* or *A Murder of Mages*.

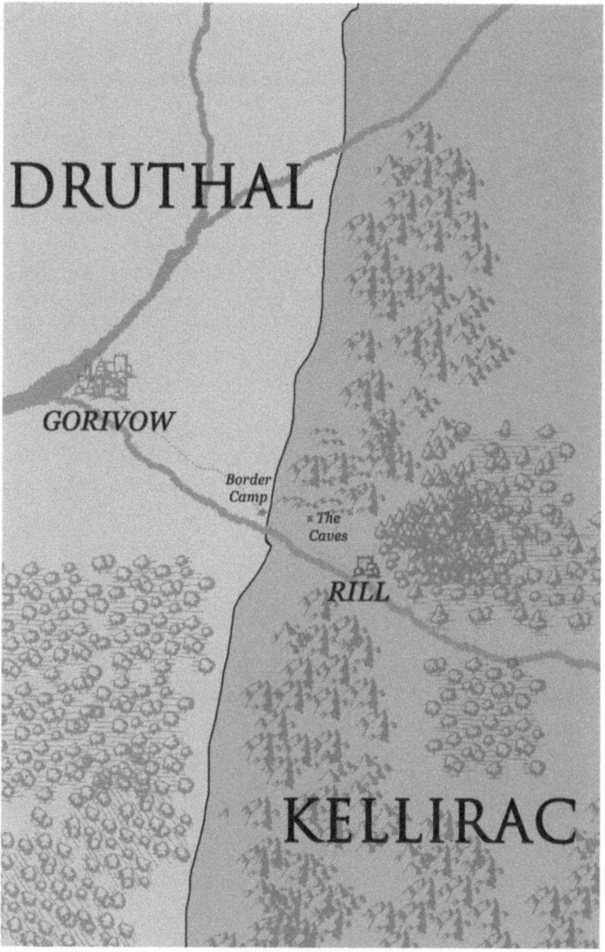
DRUTHAL
GORIVOW
Border
Camp
The
Caves
RILL
KELLIRAC

Aurien Pemmick's entire body was a shrine to his devotion—his feet calloused, every joint ached, his stomach growling with a hunger that had not been truly sated in months— while he kept a joyful smile on his face and a polite nod to everyone he passed on his slow, painful walk to the High Cathedral of Gorivow. The cathedral was a gaudy, ostentatious structure: polished stone, stained glass, grand doors inlaid with silver, all towering over a cracked and faded square of the city's threadbare market district. Given the surroundings, Pemmick was surprised to see that active construction was underway—a new wing was being added to the already immense church.

It was not his place to question it, though. He was merely a deacon on his Itinerancy, doing good works in the name of God and the saints until he was ready to be named a reverend and placed in a residency. Which was exactly why, in all likelihood, Calistair Prenton, the Bishop of Gorivow, had summoned him.

As Pemmick went in the front door, a robed friar ran up to him with disapproving waves of his hands.

"No, no, no beggars through here. The soup line starts at two bells, and is at the door on Calder Street."

"I'm not a beggar," Pemmick said amiably. "Though I can see why you would think that." As was the tradition on Itinerancy, he had travelled on foot with just one set of clothes, so he was dirty and ragged. "Deacon Aurien Pemmick, on my Walk."

"Your accent's a bit odd," the friar said. "How far has your Walk taken you?"

"However long it is from Marikar to here," Pemmick said. "Six, seven hundred miles?"

"And you have your papers?" The friar said, his face still filled with doubt.

"Of course," Pemmick took his pack off and dug out his credentials. "I also have a letter from Reverend Andale, telling me to come see the Bishop."

The friar snatched the papers out of Pemmick's hands. "We don't have an Andale here."

"He wrote to me, and I've known him for years," Pemmick said. "There's a signet seal at the bottom." It was odd, certainly, that the summons even found him on his Walk, but God and the saints must have guided it to him themselves.

"Hmm," the friar said. He glanced at the seal and the garnet ring on his own finger. "Come with me to the quarters. I will alert the bishop, but you cannot have an audience with him in this state."

"Really?" Pemmick asked. "He's never met with a deacon on the Walk?"

"It is highly irregular. Come with me."

The friar led Pemmick through a door in the corner of the entranceway— Pemmick wouldn't have noticed it had he not been brought to it— and down two flights of stairs. They came upon another friar, who the first one passed Pemmick off to. Pemmick was quietly ushered to baths and then to a sleeping cell where an acolyte's robe was laid out for him. It was the first time he had felt properly clean in months, or had bathed in something other than the Keonia River. That was the nature of Itinerancy, and it was a test of Pemmick's devotion that he was perfectly fine with. However, he didn't mind getting to put on fresh clothes, and since the Bishop's men had instructed him to do so, it wasn't a violation of his Itinerancy.

He had grown somewhat fond of the beard he had grown in the past months, but it was a monstrosity. He wasn't at all surprised that the friar had decided to trim it and comb it out. Again, since it was being done to him, it was within the rules of the Itinerancy.

Cleaned and groomed, he was shuttled over to a grand office in the rear wing of the cathedral. He sat in the ornate chair for some time before he was finally joined by the Bishop.

"Deacon," the Bishop said as he came in. He was an older man, heavyset in hands and face. "Forgive me for having you wait for so long."

"Patience is what is expected, your Grace," Pemmick said. "I have it in reserve."

The Bishop poured two cups of wine and gave one to Pemmick as he sat at his desk. "Yes, indeed. You're Itinerant right now? Walked this way from Marikar?"

"It's been quite a few months," Pemmick said, sipping at the wine. There was a warmth and luxury to it that he hadn't been allowed in a long time.

"May I ask, why did you choose to take an Itinerancy to earn your place as Reverend? Hardly anyone does that anymore."

Pemmick had been contemplating this for a while. "It isn't the easy way, true. I'm not sure why it called to me."

"But you feel it was a calling?"

"Definitely, your Grace. I simply… knew that it was my path."

"And you have a letter instructing you to come here? To seek an audience with me?"

"I do," Pemmick said, producing it. "I was quite surprised that the letter found me in the village I had come to, but there it was, waiting for me."

Bishop Prenton hummed quietly as he looked over the letter. "This is very strange. You know Reverend Andale?"

"I do. He was one of my instructors in Marikar. I haven't seen him in over a year, of course."

"Yes, hmm," the Bishop drummed his fingers on the desk, and then took a sip of his wine. "This is very irregular."

"The friar at the door said that Reverend Andale wasn't here."

"He isn't," the Bishop said. "In fact, he only spent a few days in Gorivow, about a year ago. He is technically under my charge, but…"

"But?"

"He's been on mission all this time. In Kellirac."

"Why did he write for me to come here from Kellirac?"

The Bishop nodded. "Exactly what I wonder. This is his writing. He's written to me several times since he's gone there, but…"

The Bishop clearly had a habit of trailing off mid-thought. "Something concerns you about Reverend Andale, your Grace?"

"I'm hesitant to burden you with it, Deacon, but you are here, apparently by his summons. Perhaps this is a sign from the saints themselves." He opened a drawer of his desk and started rummaging through it. "This is the last letter I received from him, two weeks ago."

He handed a letter to Pemmick. This was not Andale's usual handwriting, instead it was a mad scrawl.

Do not walk, the night is knowing.
The dead are unquiet.
This is our hand. This is our sin.
The dead are unquiet.
The dead are unquiet.
Why is it dark under the knowing moon?
The dead are unquiet
the dead are unquiet
unquiet

"That is disturbing," Pemmick said, handing the letter back.

"I wrote back, instructing him to come home, but… I fear that he might be too far gone."

"A reasonable fear," Pemmick said. "I've heard disturbing stories about Kellirac."

"Well founded stories, Deacon," the Bishop said. He took a heavy sip of his wine. "I've lived here, near the border, for most my life, and Kellirac lives up to its reputation. The people are harsh, uncivilized—"

"Truly?" Pemmick had met several Racquin— the semi-nomadic folk of Kelliracqui descent who wandered throughout Druthal. Especially during the past few months, he found them a warm, open people who welcomed him with great hospitality.

The Bishop raised an eyebrow, clearly not pleased with the interruption. "In a harsh, unruly land. The people can't quite help being what they are, as the very environment is unforgiving. Dry heat, sudden storms. I'm even told magic doesn't work rightly there, and there are… other stories."

"The dead are unquiet." Pemmick said.

"Andale has likely lost his mind," the Bishop said holding up the letter. "But I imagine there is a real cause beneath this ramble. Since you know him, perhaps you are the man to find out."

"Of course, your Grace, I will do anything to help him. And you."

"Good," the Bishop said. He took out blank paper from his desk. "As of right now I am lifting you from the bonds of your Itinerancy. I'm going to write out some orders for you to take a carriage to the encampment at the border, and from there you'll travel into Kellirac. Reverend Andale was in a town called Rill."

"So my orders are?" Pemmick asked.

"Find Andale, and find out what happened to him. Bring him home safely, if you can. You'll go in the morning, so get some rest tonight. The brothers here will see to you and whatever you need."

"I will do my best, your Grace."

The Bishop stood up and presented his ringed hand to Pemmick— far more rings than the just the traditional Ring of Office a Bishop would typically wear. Pemmick kissed the Ring of Office dutifully.

"May the saints watch over you, Deacon," the Bishop said with a gesture of his hand that made it clear it was time for Pemmick to leave his office.

Pemmick nodded and backed his way to the door. "And may we all walk with them."

2

The road to the Kellirac border was rough and rocky, and the carriage ride deeply unpleasant. Every moment, the carriage would bump and jostle, the sound of the wheels and horses so loud, Pemmick could barely keep a civil thought in his head.

He decided he needed to embrace the unpleasantness. His Itinerancy might be formally lifted, but in his mind, he was still serving it. He may not be walking, but the travel was not significantly easier at this time. And it was for a good purpose, a godly purpose. Reverend Andale might be in great need of help, so Pemmick had to believe that the saints had put him on this path for a purpose.

That was the only explanation he had for his choice to perform The Walk, a ritual to earn the full ascension to Reverend that was unheard of outside of the most extreme, ascetic orders. It was almost never done except as an act of penance. And while Pemmick's life was hardly without sin — he was still a mortal man, imperfectly made of flesh— he had no great burden on his soul that required such a hardship. But yet, his calling to perform it was powerful.

Perhaps the sins he needed to serve his penance for were the ones he had yet to commit. The saint who whispered into his heart to do The Walk must have seen it. So he bore the hardship of Itinerancy, the challenge of the Walk, because he knew he must. The carriage ride to Kellirac was much the same.

The countryside as they approached the border was increasingly dry and dusty, all the grass now yellow and dying, the road dotted with twisted, leafless trees. As the sun hung low behind them, the carriage came to a stop at an encampment—soldiers in the Druth army living in tents, and a few roughly assembled cabins right at the side of the road.

"Whoa, hold," a pike-wielding solider said, coming up to the carriage as Pemmick disembarked. "What's your business?"

"Church business, son," Pemmick said, handing over his papers. "Deacon Aurien

Pemmick, and my driver— didn't catch your name."

The carriage driver, who had barely said anything since leaving Gorivow, merely grunted and went to attend to his horses.

Pemmick turned back to the soldier. "I'm on an assignment from the Bishop of Gorivow to go into Kellirac."

"Right," the solider said. "But it's sundown, you don't want to be going across right now. Presume you'd want to bunk down with us and head in at first light."

"Just so, if I can presume to intrude on your hospitality."

Another soldier came over. "Man of God and the saints is always welcome with us, Reverend."

"Deacon," Pemmick said. "Not a reverend yet."

"Sergeant Casper, of the Sauriyan 11th," the soldier said, extending his hand. "Welcome to the border camp."

"Deacon Pemmick," he said, taking the hand. "Glad to be here."

The other soldier helped the driver lead off his horses to another part of the camp. Casper led Pemmick to the tents. "So what brings you to Kellirac?"

"There's a reverend, my former teacher, who went on mission to a town called Rill—"

"Rill, right," Casper said. "Just about ten miles off the border, right down that road. As much as you can call it a road."

"Roads in Kellirac are even worse than the one I came on?"

"Oh, yes," Casper said. "Just about everything is. Kellirac is... it's its own thing."

"It's my first time this far east," Pemmick said. "Can you explain?"

"Well, these boys are a good example." Casper pointed to a group of soldiers who seemed to be playing a game. One of them was blindfolded, and the others were hooting and jeering as he walked, hands outstretched. He took a few steps, and then stomped his foot down definitively.

"There!" he shouted, pulling off the blindfold.

"You've been in for ten paces!" another said.

Pemmick and Casper approached. "What's this then?"

The soldiers, almost all young men, suddenly snapped to attention. "Sorry, sir. Reverend. We were just—"

Pemmick didn't bother correcting them on the title. "It's fine, I'm just curious what it's all about."

"Oh, it's the border," one of them said. He

pointed to the markers— a line of flags spaced every thirty feet or so.

Pemmick wasn't sure what he was expecting, but he thought it would be more formal than that. A wall at the very least.

"You put on the blindfold and walk, and guess when you've crossed over into Rack."

"And how does that work?"

"Swear, you can feel it," another said. "There's something just strange when you go over."

Pemmick took a step in the direction of the flags cautiously stepping over the line. He wasn't sure what it was he was supposed to notice. He did feel odd, but he presumed that was just the emotions tied with the transgression. Crossing a border should be more formal, he felt, and there was dissonance in how pedestrian it was.

"If you say so," Pemmick said. "It's all land, we're all people. The Kelliracqui are just other souls in the eyes of God."

"No, it's real," the one who had been blindfolded said. "I didn't do great this time, but you can always tell when you're over the border. Always."

"Brondar always gets it perfect!" another said, pointing at one the other soldiers. "Every time!"

"It's just luck," Brondar said off-handedly.

"Every time," the other soldier said emphatically.

Pemmick nodded, not wanting to argue the point further with them. Surely, being stationed here on the border was stressful, and these boys needed some way to cope with that. "Do you all have a chaplain here? Someone to minister to your souls?"

"No such," Brondar said. "Ontarin there will read from the Book of Saints to us sometimes, and one of us will lead a blessing at chow time."

"Are you hungry, Rev?" Ontarin asked. "Saints, Sarge, we need to be hospitable to a holy man."

"True enough," Casper said.

"I'm not here to be a burden. Just passing my way to Rill."

"Never a burden, friend," Casper said. "Let's get him a hot meal and a bunk. We'll make sure you're safe to head out in the morning."

3

The ground was beyond parched. It seemed ravenous for moisture, all dried out and cracked, like the face of an angry old man. Pemmick watched the ground as his carriage drove along, pulled by two stout horses over the dusty, broken dirt road.

"Is it always this dry out here?" he asked. His driver, atop the carriage, said nothing in response. The driver had not said a single word to him since they left the army camp keep and crossed the border into Kellirac, despite Pemmick's repeated attempts to engage him.

"Has this been a drought, or is this how the season is?" He had remembered reading in his school days about Kellirac weather being strange and extreme. Sudden flooding storms with destructive winds, oppressively hot summers, bitterly cold winters. It was amazing that people lived here.

The driver continued to not respond.

Ahead on the road, three figures were walking, leading a pack animal. A donkey or a mule, Pemmick couldn't really tell the difference. The animal was loaded with bags and satchels. Farmers to market, he first thought, before looking around at the land. It didn't inspire the idea of farming, but the Kelliracs had to eat something.

He gave a courteous wave as the carriage passed them. The group was two men, one much older than the other, and a woman, though by the large, broad-shouldered bodies they all had it was difficult to tell the difference. All three wore a rough set of garments that resembled pullover shirt and skirt made out of rawhide and lined with fur, flapping in the coarse wind that was sweeping over the countryside. It struck Pemmick that it would be too hot to wear such a thing. All three of them had wide brimmed hats made of straw, resting on top of dark blond hair. The older man had streaks of grey and white in his, as well as in the large, bushy beard that threatened to take over his face.

Three sets of eyes looked up at the carriage as it went by, all making contact with Pemmick. Those eyes were filled with distrust, annoyance, and flashes of anger. The older Kellirac man glanced at the crest on the side of the carriage, an emblem of the Church and the Diocese of Gorivow, and barked at them. Pemmick couldn't make any sense of what the man was saying, though he was clearly upset. Despite the man breaking into a jog to keep up with them as he ranted, they were soon out of earshot.

"Do you know what that was about?" he asked the driver. The driver gave a noncommittal grunt as his only comment. Pemmick found that to be an encouraging improvement.

The dirt road began to run parallel to a small, trickling stream as they approached the town— Rill, Pemmick presumed, which from the distance resembled a low stone fortress, surrounded by a twisting, dying forest beyond. The driver, while remaining silent, was looking more and more troubled as he looked to the horizon, where a mass of clouds were moving closer and growing grayer with each passing moment. He shouted out to the horses, urging them faster.

The carriage was knocked about as it raced on the uneven road, the horses approaching a full gallop. Pemmick tried to hold on to the front of the seat as he pulled himself forward to get closer to the driver, but a violent jolt sent him sprawling back. He yelled, "I don't think this is wise!" before he looked back up.

The wind was howling around them, the sky covered with black clouds. They were only a few hundred yards away from the town's walls when the sky shattered open on top of them, smashing down in a torrential downpour.

The dirt road turned to mud in seconds. The horses faltered and crashed over themselves, the carriage upturned and slid over the mud towards the creek, now raging and roiling. Pemmick lost all sense of where he was or how he was moving, finding himself waist deep in the water, struggling to keep himself from being swept away.

"Driver!" he shouted. He had never even learned the man's name. He couldn't see more than a few inches through the pelting rain, barely able to even keep his eyes open. He wasn't even sure if he was moving towards the riverbank, since he had only the force of the water flow giving him any sense of direction.

"Driver!" he called again. He touched solid ground—relatively solid, at least—and struggled to scramble his way out of the creek. He had barely managed to get to his feet when he was struck hard on the shoulder, sending him crashing down into the mud. All around him, he could hear the muted thuds of large hailstones landing in the soft ground.

The only sound he could hear above the storm was a horse, screaming in panic and pain. He crawled his way over to it, while being pummeled with hail along his body.

He managed to reach the horse, placing his hand on its back. It was vainly trying to free itself, having been pinned down by the body of the other horse, which had broken its neck. The dead horse was too heavy, and the ground too slippery for the survivor to get purchase. It briefly flashed through Pemmick's thoughts that it had been extremely foolish of him to risk getting so close to the upset animal; it could easily maul him. He had no idea what he was trying to do. In his confusion, his desperation, he had locked on to the idea that his only chance to survive the next few minutes involved helping the horse.

He tried to push the dead horse off the living one, but he had neither the strength or the traction to accomplish that. He struggled, enduring wild sideswipes from the horse's leg, until one hailstone cracked him in the skull, sending him reeling.

He stumbled, dazed and bleeding. Everything left his memory: the horses, the carriage, the driver, his mission or even where he was. Only one idea pushed its way to the surface of his thoughts: *Somewhere ahead of me, there is a town, and with it, shelter.*

"Hear me, Saint Ollickar, and guide me to salvation," he whispered. In that moment, he wasn't sure if he meant for his life, or his soul beyond life, but he was determined to push himself forward, regardless.

On his feet again, he moved in what he believed was the direction of the town, calling out for someone, anyone, who could hear him. He stumbled forward, reaching his hands out, until they touched the stonework of the village wall. Feeling around, he found an entranceway, and went through it.

"Thank you, my saints," he muttered. He fell down in a secluded corner of muddy road and wall where the rain and hail weren't hitting him, losing all sense of consciousness.

4

Pemmick woke up disoriented in darkness. He was dry and inside, and had been sleeping in a cot of some sort. His body was riddled with aches, his head was dressed with a bandage, otherwise undamaged. He said a small prayer of gratitude for that.

He had been cleaned and cared for, his clothing removed and replaced with a shift made of raw, rough cloth. He was able to get out of the cot with little difficulty.

He crossed the room to the only source of light, an open window that was little more than a hole cut into the masonry of the wall. Moonslight was shining through; the small red moon nearly full, the larger white one little more than a sliver, giving a pale pink glow to the room. The room was simple, a stone floor, bare walls, and the cot he had been sleeping on its only furnishings. There was a wooden door, closed with flickering light visible through the crack underneath it. He tried the door, and was surprised that it was unlocked. Wherever he was, he was not necessarily a prisoner, unless he had careless jailers.

The door opened to a large common room. It had the same stone floor, with a roughly made wooden table and matching benches taking the center of the room. There was a ceramic stove in the corner of the room, with a small fire crackling inside it providing light. Storage cabinets lined one wall, very finely made, which Pemmick suspected were of Druth origin rather than Kellirac.

A woman came out from another back room, carrying a wooden bowl with a dark paste in it. She was definitely Kellirac, her hair put up in several small, tight braids, her dress made of leather hide and undyed cloth. She was several steps in the room before she noticed Pemmick standing there, which caused her to stop in her tracks.

"Sorry," he said, "I didn't—"

"You're awake," she said in accented Trade. She placed the bowl on the table, and went back out the way she came.

"Could you tell me—" Pemmick started, but she was already gone. Unsure of what to do, he sat down on one of the benches and looked in the bowl. Whatever it was she was mixing, it had a nauseating odor that struck him as soon as he sat near it. He pushed the bowl to the far side of the table.

The woman returned with a young man— who was somehow dark-skinned but pallid, and his short-cropped hair was shock white. "You're awake," he said. "How do you feel?"

"I've felt worse," Pemmick said. "I presume I have you to thank for my care?"

"I found you in the gateway, but Theyasa here cared for you. That was two days ago."

"Need to change the dressing," she said. She grabbed Pemmick by the shoulder and pushed him into a chair. She unwrapped the bandage on his head. While she worked, the young man sat down opposite him.

"Tell me who you are," the young man said.

"Aurien Pemmick."

"You are a priest of the Druth Church?" the young man asked him.

"I'm a deacon," he said. "I've yet to earn the full rank of Reverend."

"Hmmm," the young man said. "And why would a deacon of the Druth Church come to Rill? Come to Kellirac?"

"I'm looking for a friend of mine," Pemmick said.

"You have come here for a friend?" He looked at Pemmick with his piercing pale blue eyes. "You surely know this place is not safe, not for Druth men, not for church men. But yet you come."

"He thinks himself a holy man," the woman scoffed as she slathered the foul-smelling paste on his head.

"I think myself a man of faith, nothing more," Pemmick offered.

"He knows so little," Theyasa said. "Not recognizing a real holy man."

"Hush, Theyasa," the young man said.

"I— I had a letter," Pemmick said. Other memories came rushing back as the woman started bandaging his head. "My carriage, my driver. Did you... were they rescued?"

"I'm sorry, deacon," the young man said. "Nothing else was found."

"Nothing? There was a carriage, two horses. Surely..."

"When those storms come, the flood of the river is like— nothing you can imagine. Sudden, voracious. It probably washed away the carriage, the horses, everything in the blink of an eye. You are lucky you survived."

"The driver... he... could he have...."

The young man tilted his head as if listening to something far away. Then he looked back at Pemmick. "I wish I had more to tell you."

"Who are you, exactly?"

The young man's attention focused on Pemmick again, eyes fixed and strong. "I'm... sorry. I'm Thaun. Thaun du Rill, I'm... an *onnoukin* of this household."

"I don't know that term."

"It doesn't translate to Trade well," Theyasa said.

"You might say something like 'Not-Prince'. Except you wouldn't say that." On that, Thaun stood up abruptly and, his focus suddenly somewhere else entirely, walked out the door.

"Did... did I offend?" Pemmick asked.

"No, he's... he's like that," Theyasa said. She finished wrapping his head. "You're well enough to walk. Be out of my business. I have preparations to make. Find your own way about."

And with little ceremony, she hauled him to his feet and pushed him out the door.

5

Pemmick's first instinct was to follow Thaun, but the young man had slipped out of sight. So for several minutes, he stood dumbfounded in the Kellirac streets, unclear where he should go or what he should do next.

The gray light of dawn crept over him, as the people of the town were coming out of their homes and getting to their daily business. Realizing he looked even more conspicuous just standing about, he decided to walk and explore his surroundings. He followed the stone road to a central plaza, where he would have presumed the folks going about their business would be setting up shops and carts for the business of the day. But despite the locals all being very active, none of them were engaging in the sort of business he associated with a busy city in the morning.

He sat on a low wall and watched them for a

bit, and shortly realized they were all doing the same things. Stringing lanterns across the street. Hanging a garland of herbs and roots on the windows. Setting small breads and other foods at their doorsteps.

Rituals. Preparations. That was the word Theyasa had used. Was this a holiday?

"Pardon me?" he asked one man who passed by him. "Is this a special day of some sort?"

"Ah yes, don't ya know?" he said, his accent almost indecipherably thick. "It's Hultichia, you know."

"I do not, in fact," Pemmick said. "And Hultichia means?"

"It's the night of the dead, friend. They walk tonight. You have a place to stay behind a door?"

"I… am not sure."

"Then you best be finding a place, friend. You do not want to be a-street when the dead are walking. Or, by Jox and Javer, nothing might preserve you."

Pemmick wasn't sure what to make of that, but he decided it was not worth arguing. "Can you point me to someone in authority? An official, perhaps a sheriff?"

"Saw the Lord himself heading out the gate to the field houses," the man said, pointing down the road. "Just a few breaths ago, so you could still catch him up."

The Lord? Pemmick found it almost incredulous that the noble ruling this town would just wander out the gate, and that this man would know him, would speak of him so casually. In twenty years growing up in Marikar, he never once saw the Duke, or almost any of the city's nobility. Still, he might as well see for himself.

"Thank you, sir," he said. He refrained from adding a blessing. It was unlikely this fellow, with his superstitions of the dead walking and Jox and Javer, would appreciate it.

Pemmick took the road, past the townfolk continuing to ornament their windows and doors. A fascinating bit of ritual, and he was grateful that, if nothing else, he would be able to study this holiday and the faith of these people up close. Truly, these charms and offerings were not that different from the prayer tokens the Druth faithful would leave at the feet of the saints' statues.

He crossed out of the gate— which, to his surprise, was just open and unguarded. He had expected at least some form of watch in place. Once he was outside, it was clear that nearly the entire town was inside the walls. There were some structures backed right up to the wall, but mostly it was grain fields and muddy roads. Not too far away, a group of locals were working on repairing a squat building, which must have been damaged in the storm. Pemmick approached the group, who were all stripped to the waist, with wide-brimmed straw hats that kept the hard sun off their faces.

"Hello!" he called out. "Apologies for disruption, I'm looking for someone who is in charge?"

"He means you," one of the men said, slapping another of the shirtless men on the arm.

"Eh, yeah," that one— an older fellow with gray-streaked hair and beard. "You're that Druth fellow who almost got killed in the storm."

"And I appreciate you and yours saving me."

"Mine," he said with a scoff. "I had nothing to do with it. My half-son insisted on bringing you in, so I did not forbid it. I thought you'd die and it would be a waste of energy to save you. But I am glad you're on your feet."

"Yes, doing much better," Pemmick said. He offered his hand. "Deacon Aurien Pemmick."

"Falto du Rill," the man said, grabbing Pemmick by the forearm. "Steadholder of Rill. You are welcome to the steading, seeing how it is a sacred day, but do not abuse my hospitality."

This was the noble lord of this town, and here

he was, taking Pemmick's hand, working with his people, as if he was no different than any other man. Fascinating to see. Most Druth folk of any station would faint dead away at the idea of such humility.

"I never would with intention," Pemmick said. "If I may ask?"

Falto turned back to the work of reattaching the broken door. "Don't waste my time with asking to ask. Say your mind."

"I came here in search of an old friend, a Reverend Andale? I received a letter that he might be in trouble."

"I don't know much about that. Heyo! Any of you all know about a Druth man named Andale?"

"Oy, that priest fellow, boss," someone called out. "That was what he was called."

"Right, him," Falto said, scratching his beard. "That fellow, think he left weeks ago. Definitely gone, probably dead."

"Dead?" Pemmick asked. "Is there… can we be sure?"

"You can maybe ask a *thikaavh*, they might have a message."

"A what?"

"Maybe your priest friend will knock tonight!" someone called out. "You never know who the dead will seek."

"I'm sorry?"

Falto stopped his work and turned to Pemmick, putting a beefy hand on his shoulder. "Listen, friend, we have much to do, and only so much daylight. You are welcome to the steading, but if you have any sense, you'll go back to where you woke up and stay inside until dawn tomorrow. Theyasa will take care of you. Now please stop being a nuisance, at least to me and my people."

6

Pemmick found his way back to the house he woke up in, after some purposeful wandering. Now that he got a sense of the layout of the town, it was clear it was designed as a series of expanding circles, with the stronghold in the center. Rill wasn't just surrounded by walls, but several sets of walls, creating layers of town encircling the stronghold. The house he woke up in was in the innermost circle, part of the Steadholder's grounds.

The door was shut, but the stoop outside had several breads, cakes and pies set out, and the windows were shuttered with the garlands of herbs and flowers hanging in front. He knocked on the door, not wanting to presume to just come inside without warning.

After a moment, he heard nothing, and knocked again louder.

The door flew open, and Theyasa glared at him, her face filled with horror. Then she scowled at him.

"It's you," she said dismissively, coming away from the door. "You gave me a terror knocking like that. On this day of all days."

"Sorry," Pemmick said. "I was told to come back here, that I should be inside before the sun set."

"You absolutely should, but you cannot— who told you?"

"The Steadholder."

She sighed. "Of course. Then you will be welcome in these doors. But do not be a disruption."

"I have no intention of being a disruption," he said, coming inside.

"That last Druth priest was always a disruption. Stuck his nose in everything."

"The last— You knew Reverend Andale?"

"Was that his name? Aye, I knew him."

"I came here to find him. The Steadholder said he went missing, probably dead."

"I would not be surprised. He was a troubled man."

Pemmick knew he had to find more. "Where did he stay? Maybe I can find some clue…"

"He had a shack by the west gate."

"Can you show me?"

"I am *not* going out in the streets today, certainly not risking getting stuck out of doors when the sun sets by going across town."

Pemmick didn't have time for this superstitious nonsense. "Just tell me how to find it."

"Go west until you reach the gate. Then look for a shack with that ring you wear around your neck over the door." She meant his prayer necklace, with the incomplete circle that was the symbol of the Druth church.

Andale's shack was his church.

"Thank you," he told her, and went back out.

"If you have any sense, you'll get inside after dark!" she shouted after him.

The main thing Pemmick noticed as he made his way to the west gate was every house and shop was closed up and shuttered, with food on the stoop and charms on the windows. This holiday, this "Hultichia," was something they took seriously.

At the gate, the shack was easy to spot, marked with the unfinished circle. It was also completely run down, the door hanging off the hinges, the windows broken. Pemmick dared to go inside, and found nothing that didn't match his expectations of disappointment. No sign anyone had been here for weeks. Shambles.

Pemmick left the shack, unsure of how to proceed, unsure of how he could even return back to Gorivow. The carriage was gone, as was the driver. *That poor man, probably lost in the river*. Pemmick said a quiet prayer for him, and for Andale.

Looking up from his prayer, he noticed a group of people standing in a line, waiting with anxious patience. It had been the first time all day that he had seen any of the locals being still. They had all been so active, racing about, preparing their rituals and superstitions, it was shocking to see a group of them just standing there.

They were lined up next to a small structure, like a garden gazebo with a wall bisecting it. But there was something about it that put Pemmick in the mind of... reverence. Especially the way the people waiting stood back while one woman knelt in front of the small window in the wall, whispering and crying.

"Sorry," Pemmick said, approaching one fellow in the line. "May I ask what's going on?"

"A Caller has come to let the dead speak to those who come."

"Is this part of the holiday?" Pemmick asked. "Because the dead will walk tonight?" He tried to

keep any sounds of mockery out of his tone. He
hoped he had succeeded.

"They will. But maybe, if we can talk to them
now, things might be settled so they won't knock."

What had Theyasa said about knocking?
Someone else did as well. "The dead knocking…
is bad?"

"What sort of daft are you?" the man asked.
"Oh, you're one of them Druth fools. Well, you'll
see. And you best hope no one knocks for you."

Pemmick scowled and walked away, stepping
far enough from the shrine to see on the other
side of the wall.

The man on the other side, talking through
the window, was Thaun du Rill. The strange
young man from this morning.

He looked up and saw Pemmick, and stopped
talking to the woman. He came out from the
shrine, almost stumbling as he walked right up to
Pemmick. He stretched out his hand, nearly
touching Pemmick's face…

And then he recoiled away, pulling his whole
arm in close to his body. Tears sprang from his
eyes, and he ran off, out the west gate.

The folks in line all shook their heads, looking
more resigned than upset, and dispersed, leaving
Pemmick even more confused about what had just
happened.

Pemmick went back into Andale's shack. There was nothing but mess and chaos, but this had been his old friend's home, his things. If nothing else, Pemmick owed it to Andale, as well as devotion to faith and duty, to put Andale's possessions and space in order. If he was, as Pemmick feared, already dead, this might give a small amount of peace and closure to his life.

He set to work, clearing out the rotten and molding food, shaking out the bedding, and finding place and order to the shack. This was meant to be a holy space, on some level, a home for worship. Pemmick would make it suitable to that end, even only he would practice his faith here, and only for a small time.

Did it need to be a small time? The purpose of taking an Itinerancy was to walk and find the purpose that faith called you to. Perhaps his walk was supposed to lead him here. Perhaps his calling was to take up the ministry left behind by Reverend Andale.

But it was inappropriate to just claim a ministry, and inappropriate for a deacon to take a burden on his own shoulders like that. No, he had been sent here with a mission, assigned by the bishop, and at least completing that had to come first. He could not just presume Andale was dead, not just presume to step into the man's place.

Perhaps God, the saints, or even the bishop had another purpose for him.

First things first. Clean and clear this blessed house. Write to the bishop of what he has found so far. Keep searching for answers.

He went to the desk, deeply troubled to see Andale's copy of *The Testaments of the Saints* had been cut up, pages ripped out, the paper torn into pieces. Had these Kellirac people done this to the sacred text? Or had Andale, in the same troubled madness that drove him to write that letter, been the one who had desecrated the book?

Some of the torn-out pages had additional ink scribbled over them. Over and over, in the same wild scrawls of the letter, it was written *The forest knows what happens. The forest holds it.*

That wasn't just written on the papers, but on the desk itself, the ink set into the wood. What had gripped Andale so that he would do that?

One more sheet of paper with the same phrase, again and again, lay under the mess, but when Pemmick flipped it over, it was a map.

The city, the road from the border, the river along the road, the fields of grain outside the walls, and to the west: a forest. And marked within that forest, in an ink that matched the scrawling madness, a line showing a path, and a circle several times in a spot within the forest.

Pemmick wasted no time, taking up this map and heading out the west gate. The forest, he could see, wasn't too far from the gate, a walk of no more than a quarter hour. If the scale of the map was at all trustworthy—a premise he acknowledged was likely faulty, but he had faith— it would be another quarter hour to follow the path to the spot marked. There was daylight enough to make it out there and be back in the city walls before sunset, or close enough into dusk.

Not that he took the superstitious fears of Theyasa and the others seriously. Surely, the dark could be dangerous, but nothing he needed to worry too much about.

The path through the woods, the trees dry and twisted, rough bark and tangled, thorny vines draped between each half-dead tree, was subtle. It had obviously been formed by people taking the same route through here for years, if not generations, but not so well trafficked that it didn't have scrub and leaves obscuring it as he made his way through. He had spent enough time as a boy making his way from his family's cabin to the nearby villages and back to track a rough path in the woods.

The path opened up to a small glade, dappled with the rosy orange light of the setting sun casting long shadows of the twisted trees. Looking back at the map, it seemed clear, this was the spot that had been circled. What was here, what had Andale's attention that he would mark it on the map?

Then he saw: a mound of loose earth, recently dug, marked with a stone. Resting on the stone was a necklace, an unfinished circle like the one Pemmick wore, and a wooden board with the words *Reverend Finvy Andale, Rest Under the Gaze of the Saints.*

Pemmick dropped to his knees, allowing himself to cry and pray for his old friend. It shattered his heart to confirm that he was dead, but it was good, at least, that someone had taken the care to bury him properly and mark him with a blessing of his faith.

But who would do that? Who, in this place of superstitious heathens, would honor him this way?

Pemmick heard footsteps behind him, and turned to see the answer.

"I'm so very sorry," Thaun du Rill said, tears streaming down his face. "I know how much he loved you."

7

Pemmick stood stunned, unable to even understand what Thaun du Rill had just said.

"He wanted you—"

"Wait, what?" Pemmick exploded. "How did you… why do you…" He finally just pointed to the grave. "Is this you? Did you do this?"

"I did," Thaun said, kneeling in front of the grave. "I thought it might give him some rest, but…"

"How did you know him?"

"I honestly didn't, not while he was alive."

Pemmick had no idea what to make of that. "But you said—"

"I was aware of him, of course. Especially since he placed his hut next to one of the calling shrines. I wish he hadn't done that, of course. I thought it was very disrespectful."

"That's where you were talking to those people through the window?" Pemmick asked. He presumed it was another aspect of the Kellirac faith. It looked not unlike the Rite of Absolution, actually.

"It's one of the places in the town for that. It's... I'm..."

"Thaun, are you also a priest?"

Thaun looked up at Pemmick. "I don't know if I would use that word. It... not like he was. Or you. There's no texts or preaching, but... I'm a *thikaavh*."

"A what?"

"I commune with the dead. They call out to me, they speak through me..."

"That is nonsense, the dead are gone, called back to God and the infinite."

"The dead are always with us, they live on in our hearts," Thaun said. His eyes softened, a smile spread across his face as he reached out, touching Pemmick on his cheek. "Look how handsome you've grown, Auri. You've grown so much."

Pemmick stumbled away from him. No one had called him Auri, but... and the tone of Thaun's voice, the expression on his face... it was impossible.

"Nona?" he asked.

"Just for a moment," Thaun said rubbing his

temple. "I'm sorry, it comes in sudden bursts, and I can't get a hold of it. Especially tonight."

"Because it's, what, Hultichia? Whatever that is?"

"Take the dead seriously, Deacon," Thaun said. "And when they are angry—"

"The dead are not angry or—"

"The dead are unquiet!" Thaun snapped. "Always in my head, they want and clamor with a hunger that would make you fall down and weep. It would shatter your mind, Deacon, to hear them day and night as I do."

"You don't seem shattered."

"I've never been whole," Thaun said. "But something shattered your friend. And he was killed, out here. He called to me, and I buried him, thinking that would... that would give him..."

"He was killed?" Pemmick asked. "By who?"

"He wouldn't... couldn't tell me. The dead are often so confused, especially those who died in..."

"In what?"

"Agony."

Pemmick stormed away from this absurd, infuriating young man. "I won't hear any more of this madness."

"This madness is coming!" Thaun shouted,

chasing after him. "The sun is almost set, we need to get inside."

"Because the dead will walk?" Pemmick shouted, turning back around.

"Yes!" Thaun said. "And that is…" He stopped, realization crossing his face. "That is why he wanted you here."

"What?"

"That letter that brought you here! Written by my hand, guided by his voice!" Thaun charged up to Pemmick, grabbing him by the front of his cassock. "For whatever reason, the one thing he wanted, what he needed as he screamed to me from death, was for you to come here. He wanted you to come and find him."

8

Thaun looked up to the sky, a deep purple of dusk. "We need to go now."

"But, what about Andale, what about—"

Thaun starting walking, holding onto Pemmick's cassock, dragging him as he went. "We cannot waste any time. When the sun is down—"

"Nothing will happen!" Pemmick said, trying to wrench himself free of Thaun's grip. But the boy had an arm like iron, pulling him along the path, out of the forest. "If you don't let me go—"

That was all Pemmick managed before Thaun lifted him up and threw him over his shoulder, breaking into a run. As they crossed the field from the forest to the town, a howling wind kicked up the dust, clouding Pemmick's vision further as the last streams of red and orange cut through the western sky. It was impossible to see anything beyond the walls once they passed the gate and Thaun put Pemmick back on his feet.

"I don't know who you think you are," Pemmick said. "But it is very unseemly to handle another man like that."

"We have no time to lose, we must get inside. If we hurry back to my lodge, Theyasa has already—"

"I'm not going anywhere. If I must stay somewhere for the night, I'll stay in Andale's church right here. I'll at least…"

"No!" Thaun shouted. "The door is gone, nothing is warded, you won't be safe, and—"

"Safe from what? You think the dead will be walking through the streets or something?"

"Yes, you foolish Druth man!" Thaun said. "Exactly that!"

"Madness! That is impossible!"

Thaun took a step back and a deep breath. "You are so certain of that, it is incredible. You do not know what this night is. You don't know where you are." His voice and demeanor shifted. "You are making yourself a victim of your own closed mind, Mister Pemmick." He pointed one finger with a definitive tremor in his hand that put Pemmick immediately in mind of being back in seminary class.

Exactly how Reverend Andale would when he was teaching.

It was exactly the thing Andale would say. The very phrase.

Thaun turned around and started walking, as if he knew he had argued his point as much as he needed, and he was right. Pemmick hurried along after him. They both doubled their pace as they passed shut door after shut door, every household closed up, food on the stoop. As they raced through town, Pemmick idly wondered if they expected the dead to eat the food, and what they imagined the consequences would be if there was none out there.

They reached the lodge of the main stronghold, where the door was already shut. Thaun slammed into the door, struggling to open it, but it had clearly been barred already.

"Theyasa!" he shouted. "Let us in!"

Somewhere behind them, Pemmick heard a sound, like metal scraping across stone, a sound that ran through his spine. Then another, another, again, again.

Pemmick felt a chill of cold sweat as a sound that *surely* was just the wind howling through the street behind them.

He heard those scraping sounds grow closer, louder, and he did not dare turn around to see.

It's just foolish local legends. Ludicrous superstition.

Theyasa opened the door, bright candlelight dancing inside.

Driven by fear and instinct, Pemmick rushed forward with Thaun, and they tumbled into the house. Theyasa shut the door and barred it.

"Foolish boys," she said derisively.

The howling still echoed outside. Pemmick felt his heart pounding in his chest, even as he berated himself for acting so foolishly. A little wind, probably a branch dragging or a sign scraping in the wind, and he was awash with fright. He had let these Kellriac people, with their foolish beliefs, get inside his head.

Still, he was glad to be inside, a warm home with a fire.

"You know better, my grace," Theyasa told Thaun. "You let this fool wrap you up."

"He is what I was called for," Thaun said. "I brought him here, he is my responsibility."

"He is yours," Theyasa said. "I will not risk myself for some Druth priest."

"I'm just a deacon," Pemmick said, still finding his breath.

"Have you eaten since this morning?" Thaun said. "Theyasa, what do you have?"

She grunted and went into the back room,

coming out quickly with wooden bowls filled with a steaming soup. Thaun sat down on the bench and gestured to Pemmick to do the same. Pemmick found that his legs were still shaking as he sat down.

"I don't supposed you could explain yourself, now that we're settled in here," Pemmick asked as he started on his soup. It had a rich and complex flavor, which Pemmick found incredibly unpleasant, but he was also ravenous, so he kept eating.

"I've told you—"

"This morning, I told you who I was, and that I was looking for my friend, and you acted like you knew nothing about such a thing."

"I should not have done that," Thaun said.

"Given that you wrote the letter."

"My hand held the pen," Thaun said. "But it was your friend Andale who wrote it."

Sophistry, Pemmick thought, but no need to dwell. "So why did you lie this morning?"

"I am not a master of my own mind," Thaun said. "The dead, they constantly hum and buzz at me, and that can... it can leave me in great separation from the world around me at times. I don't always react the way I should."

"It's why his father will barely speak to him," Theyasa offered.

"Theyasa!"

"It's true!" she said.

"You called yourself a 'not-prince' before. You are Lord Rill's son, yes?"

"I am," Thaun said. "But my mother is not his Noted Wife, but from the several among his court of consorts. And as she— and thus I— are of foreign blood, we are only regarded with the titles of outsiders." Pemmick took that in. Thaun was darker skinned than most of the other Kells, and Pemmick had heard that many refugees had fled Ch'omikTaa, crossed the desert and made homes for themselves here in Kellirac. Thaun's mother was likely from there.

Now it was clear, Thaun was a troubled young man. Hearing voices, presuming them to be the dead talking to him. This culture humored such things, treating him as a holy man.

But maybe this was the path Pemmick was supposed to be on. He was summoned here, and if not for Andale— may he rest under the saints' gaze—then perhaps to tend to the soul of Thaun du Rill.

"So, what did Andale want to tell me, then? Why did he want me here?"

"Something had so deeply troubled him, that it broke him," Thaun said. "The dead come tonight, but they are always around us here.

Perhaps they whispered to him and he went mad. Perhaps he learned something so terrible, no man could keep his mind."

"And you don't know what?"

"Even dead, he is troubled. That stays with him and his words, filled with madness. When he speaks, I can barely—" Thaun paused, his hand to his chest. He struggled to catch his breath. "But the truth is coming."

"What truth?"

As he said this, there was a sharp rap at the door. Three knocks, slowly pounded out with determination.

Theyasa screamed and dropped the bowl she was holding. "The Dead have come to us!"

"Stop it," Pemmick scolded. He stood up and crossed to the door. "Who's there? If someone is playing some sort of jape, it is not appreciated."

Three more hard, slow knocks.

"The dead knock!" Theyasa said. "They have come for one of us and we must answer."

"Easy!" Pemmick said.

Thaun quietly crossed to the door. "There's no use in ignoring. When they come, we answer. Who they come for must follow."

"Are you having me on?" Pemmick asked.

Thaun opened up the door, and Pemmick was

shocked to see he recognized who was on the other side.

The carriage driver.

"Well, old boy, you made it," he said. "I was worried you had been——"

Pemmick stopped short once he saw the man better. The driver had a grey pallor, his hair was matted down with caked blood and dirt, and the side of his head was gashed open. A wound like that, no man could get up from.

Wordlessly, the driver pointed to Pemmick, stooped down to pick up a loaf of bread on the doorstep, and turned and walked off.

"The Dead chose you," whispered Theyasa, "You have to follow him."

"I'd follow him to help the poor man," Pemmick said. "He must be addled from having his brains smashed." He ran out into the night, with Thaun right at his heels.

The driver, despite his stumbling gait, was already well down the street and headed out past the town walls when they spotted him. They ran to catch up with him.

"Driver!" Pemmick called, but the man did not react or stray from his determined walk. "Where is he going?"

"Wherever he goes, he chose you. Do not risk

what might happen if you don't follow," Thaun said.

"You can't think— that man isn't dead, Thaun."

"You must follow," Thaun said. Pemmick noticed the young man was now carrying a mason hammer. "But I will not leave your side. We will see what the dead have to tell you."

9

The night was filled with moving shadows as Pemmick followed the silent driver out of the city. He didn't see anyone else in the streets, but always there was movement out of the corner of his eye, the sounds of scraping footsteps, and the inhuman howls of the wind.

"Is this what this night is always like?" he asked Thaun.

"This is the first time I've dared to be in the streets on Hultichia," Thaun said. "No one does unless the dead knock for them, and they…"

"They what?" Pemmick asked, fearing the answer would be "never come back."

"Keep their experience to themselves," Thaun said. "Being called by the dead is very personal, very sacred."

"But you came with me."

"It's not a part of your sanctity," Thaun said. "And I can't quite *hear* your friend Andale right now, but I can feel him, and…" He trailed off.

"And what?" Pemmick asked, as they continued down an almost abandoned trail, leading around the tangled forest, further and further west.

"It feels like a warning. He doesn't want you to be alone."

"I must admit, I am grateful for the company. Besides, you know, that fellow…" He pointed to the driver, continuing his long, tireless walk through the moonslit night. "…Not much of a talker."

The walk kept going, long into the night, for miles. Still, the incessant howling of the wind never ended.

"Where even are we?" Pemmick asked. "Are you familiar with this place?"

"Not particularly. I know there are some villages out this way, between here and the border," Thaun said. "But it all feels… anguished."

Pemmick didn't know how to parse that. "In what way?"

Thaun put his hand on the ground, closing his eyes. "I'm not sure, it's dulled but… this is a place of sorrow. So many… oh."

"What?"

He got up and continued the walk. "We are near the border with your nation. This land was again and again a place of dispute. So many have died here over the centuries, it's drenched with the dead."

"I'm sorry," Pemmick said.

"The guilt of these dead, the guilt of nations, cannot be borne on the shoulders of two men. And I've found that often the dead do not blame the living."

"No?" Pemmick asked. That was surprising.

"Some do, but most are made of regret. Those that reach out through me, for the most part, are trying to lay down that regret. Often, it's just to say the things they were afraid to in life."

"This fellow never said a word to me in his life," Pemmick said. "Really, our relationship hasn't changed."

"The dead who come on this night, they're not the ones who speak to me. When the dead knock for you on Hultichia, it's because you have to do something."

"A holy task laid on me?" Pemmick asked. "That's already what I've been doing, walking until I find the calling God has placed on me. I don't mind walking a little more." Whatever this was, wherever he was being led— be this the path of God or Kellirac superstition, he would greet it and rise to it as best he could. His faith demanded no less.

The journey led them into a ravine— they couldn't be more than a couple miles from the border now— and as they reached the bottom, the driver finally stopped walking. He glanced back at them for the first time, and with a gesture to follow, entered a cave in the wall of the cliff face.

"Do you know what this is?" Pemmick asked. "Where we are?"

"I think I do," Thaun said. "I think I understand, but you... you need to see it."

Pemmick accepted this— he had come this far — and went in. The moonslight only extended into the mouth of the cave, the rest of it was pitch black. He stared down into the darkness, hoping to make out a bit of shadow or movement. He breathed deliberately and slowly, trying to ease the pounding beat of his heart. He could still hear Thaun at his back, feel the warmth of the young man's body.

"Driver?" he called out, "You in here?"

There was a scrape. Pemmick jumped as he saw sparks skitter across the ground, metal on stone. Then it happened again. And again. The sparks ignited into flame, which were caught on a small piece of cloth. Pemmick saw the cloth held by the driver, who used it to light a lamp he held in his other hand.

Then he saw the rest of the cave.

Bones. Skulls. So many of them, lining the floor. More bodies than he could count, still dressed in tattered rags.

And chains. Every one of these bodies had chains on their wrists and feet.

"What is this?"

"This is where I was called, Aurien," Thaun said. Thaun said it, but his tone, his voice, it was entirely Reverend Andale. "I didn't understand it at first, when I came here. Whispers in the night, voices that interrupted my prayers." Thaun walked in front of Pemmick, and everything about the way he moved had changed.

"Are you saying the dead called to you, Thaun, or—"

"It's me, Aurien," Thaun said. "The callings I heard— not unlike what this young Kell boy hears every day— it drove me wild. I didn't understand, until I came here and saw it, saw what you're seeing, that I understand who was calling me. Why they were. And even then, I couldn't handle it and live."

"What are you saying?"

"Don't make my mistake," Thaun said. "This, seeing this, realizing what it meant, it shook me so that I took my own life."

"No," Pemmick said, not even believing he was having a conversation with Reverend Andale. This was absurd. "Andale would never—"

"I was already quite mad. It was too late for me. But you, young man, sturdy soul, on the hard path that most wouldn't take... I knew you could see this truth for what it was."

"What truth?"

Thaun spoke, now as himself. "This was a silver mine. These poor folk were enslaved, forced to work in the mine, dig silver until they dropped dead of exhaustion. And when the mine was exhausted, those that sought to plunder this place — this land we fought and died for— they killed the rest and left them here."

"Who sought to plunder this place?" Pemmick asked.

"Your answer is there." Thaun pointed to one body, the bony hand wrapped around something that gleamed in the lamplight.

"What is that?" Pemmick asked absently, prying the dead fingers open. The hand was clutched around a ring. Pemmick took it and turned it over in his hand, immediately recognizing the emblem on it. The emblem of the Church and the Diocese of Gorivow.

"But—" was all Pemmick could say before the bony hand shot up and grabbed his wrist.

10

Pemmick stumbled back, but the hand kept its grip on his wrist. Then the whole skeletal body rose to its feet, its empty mouth gaping open.

"No!" Thaun shouted, bringing his hammer down on the bony arm, shattering it. But still the skeleton lurched forward, trying to grab Pemmick. Thaun put himself in between Pemmick and it, bringing down his hammer.

"What, I—" was all Pemmick could say, fear keeping breath out of him. This was impossible. All of this was impossible.

More skeletons began to rise. Slowly, methodically, all turning their empty eyes on him. The driver pointed at Pemmick and opened his mouth, an unholy scream filling the cave.

"Go, go!" Thaun yelled. "Stand down, restless

ones! Do not force me to—" His voice changed, and he turned to Pemmick, his eyes black. "*Curse befall the servants of the church! Curse befall the greedy ones—*"

Thaun shook his head, his eyes returning to normal, and swung his hammer down on another skeleton. "Do not befoul me! You do not get to have me!"

Pemmick ran out of the cave, terror filling his heart, screaming as he ran. Sense and reason left him.

But only for a moment. Forcing his courage back into himself, he stopped, calling back. "Thaun! Thaun, get out of there! Thaun!"

Thaun came running out of the cave, his clothing torn, scrapes along his dark face. "We must go. We must hurry and—"

He was interrupted by the pounding of a dozen feet rushing at them. Hands grabbed at Pemmick, pulling him away, as more figures charged at Thaun. Pemmick thrashed at his captors, trying in vain to get free.

"You won't take us, villains, Saint Ollickar will strike you—"

"Hey, hey, deacon!" a voice said. "Ease off, ease off."

Pemmick looked, and in the dark of fading

moonlight, saw that it was not some other skeletal beast, but a man. A Druth man in uniform, one he had seen before.

"Sergeant Casper?" he asked as the memory came back to him.

"Hey, Deacon," Casper said calmly. "We're here, don't worry."

"The dead," Pemmick said. "In the cave, the skeletons rose up, came at us."

"He's in a bad way," one of the soldiers said. "We got to get him back to camp."

"The skeletons!"

"They really got to him," another said. "This one probably." He went over to the other soldiers who had grabbed hold of Thaun, and grabbed the boy by the chin and dragged him over.

"Don't hurt him," Pemmick said. "He's the one who saved me."

"He'd want you to think that," Casper said. "It's what they do a lot of the time. Get in your head. Spook you with some spectre stories. Then play some trick to make you see things, and—"

"No," Thaun said. "That is not what happened."

"Shut it!" the soldier who held his face said. He let go and cracked his fist across Thaun's face.

"Stop it!" Pemmick said.

"Ease it down, Brondar," Casper ordered. "We'll take him in, and get the Deacon back safe."

"Take him in?" Pemmick asked.

"We've got holding cells for the 'racs who pull these things. Don't you worry."

"Remember what you saw, Aurien," Thaun said, his voice changing to Reverend Andale again. "Remember what you found."

"Let me just put him down," Brondar said.

"No!" Pemmick shouted. "Listen, he... he's the son of the Lord of Rill. You would cause too much trouble if you took him or hurt him."

"This dark one is the Lord's son?" Casper asked with a shrug. "You sure?"

"I am," Pemmick said. "Let him go and let's return to your base."

"Send him running," Casper ordered. Brondar scowled, and threw Thaun on the ground.

"Get gone, 'rac," he said.

Thaun got up, and looked and Brondar with an odd regard, rage in his eyes but his face calm. "The next time we meet, Joshea Brondar, will be a day of your great regret."

"I'll show you," Brondar said, pulling his sword half out of its scabbard.

Thaun stepped back, gave Pemmick one last look and said, "Remember."

He ran off into the night.

"Come on," Casper said, leading Pemmick away from the ravine as the company of the Sauriyan 11th took position around them. "Let's get you some water, maybe something to eat as we head back. Have one of the yellowshields take a look at you."

Pemmick took the offered canteen gratefully and drank down greedily. "Thank you, sergeant, I just—" Some reason and rationality came back to him. "Wait, how are you here?"

"We heard you screaming, and we moved in to help. It's what we do."

"Yes, but… why were you out here? We're a few miles from your border camp."

"Not too far, but we've been on patrol looking for you, Deacon. We were near certain you were dead."

"Why would you have thought that?"

"The creek that passes by our camp. When the flood water receded this morning, we found the remains of your carriage and the driver's body."

"The driver's— no, that's not possible."

"Menkin and Ontarin there said it was him," Casper said, pointing to two of the soldiers. "Night you spent in our camp, he talked their ear off."

It wasn't possible. He had seen the driver. He had seen what he had seen in that cave. Thaun du

Rill had been… and shown him… he had *been* Andale. And…

Pemmick looked in his hand, which he realized had been clutched tight all this time.

He had that ring. That was real.

That was proof.

11

P emmick had spent several days 'recovering' at the border camp with the Sauriyan 11th, before being delivered to Gorivow for further recuperation at the High Cathedral. He kept insisting that he was quite all right, he did not need further coddling, and requesting audience with the bishop.

He was not listened to for many days.

He spent those days exploring the High Cathedral, noting the elaborate craftwork in the wood and tiling, the candle sconces, intricacies and details everywhere, not to mention the shear scope of the expansion being built. There was quite a bit of money being spent on this cathedral.

Pemmick also noticed that quite a bit of those elaborate intricacies were silver-gilt.

After a week, he was finally called in to see the bishop.

"Ah, Pemmick," Bishop Prentin said as he came in. "I hope our hospitality and ministrations have helped you completely recover from your ordeal."

"I've been 'recovered' for some time, your grace."

"I imagine it may seem that way," the bishop said, waving for Pemmick to sit with him at a small table. Pouring out wine for the both of them. "But it's best, when having gone through a trauma like yours in Kellirac, to take more than enough time for the initial horror of it to fade away."

"It was a horror I saw," Pemmick said. "But the memory will not fade."

"I can imagine," the bishop said. "Has anyone explained to you what happened to you out there?"

"I'm aware of what happened to me. And it was terrifying, but—"

The bishop held up a finger to silence him. "So, no, they have not."

"With all due respect, your grace, what I saw out there—"

"Is not something you can trust. The Kellirac are experts in deception, it's baked into their superstitious theology. 'The dead will walk, the dead will speak'…"

"I saw—"

"What did you see?" the bishop asked. "Yes, I've read what you reported to the soldiers, as well as my brothers here. One of their 'death-callers' took you in, acted evasive about things until you confronted him, and then took you to 'find' something he wanted to show you. It is an elaborate ruse, one they are known for."

"No, no," Pemmick said. "He could *become* Andale. He was—"

"They're very gifted. Pretending to be 'channelling' the dead, especially someone they've already met? A simple act. I bet this fellow did something else where he used an affectionate name from your childhood?"

"Yes…" Pemmick said.

"One that was probably actual simplicity to guess. A perfect trap to then pull you deeper in."

"But, no, I saw the driver. I saw the skeletons come after me."

"Let me ask you," the bishop said. "Was this before or after you ate something they gave you that night?"

"After."

"Mmmm." The bishop nodded. "They have various plants that, when prepared correctly, make you see things that aren't there. They use them in their own rituals. But they probably spent the entire day telling you, 'look out, the dead will walk tonight!'"

"Yes…"

"And then feed you a broth, and what amazement! You saw the dead walk!"

"I found Andale's grave before that," Pemmick said. "I saw that he had been buried…"

"You found that despite the Kelliracs, no?"

"Yes, and—"

"All the more reason they needed to trick you. You had discovered he had been killed."

"They said he took his own life, having gone mad…"

"Perhaps true," the bishop said. "Perhaps they drove him mad, like they were trying to do to you. Perhaps they killed him. The point is, you have confirmed that Reverend Andale is, in fact, dead, and we do not need to risk further trouble by sending you or anyone else in there to determine the truth."

"The truth?" Pemmick asked. "But what about the silver mine? The dead bodies. The ring— the ring of your diocese!" Pemmick put the ring on the table.

The bishop picked it up and turned it over in his hands. "Honestly, I can't say. Of course, over the years there has been many an incident between us and the Kells, and the exact border has moved several times over the years, especially recently. Have our people dug silver out of these hills? Yes, of course. Have Kells died digging out silver? Surely."

"But we, sir— did we enslave and kill them for silver?"

The bishop sipped his wine. "Aurien," he said calmly. "You have been through quite a lot. Now, you chose to go on an Itineracy to find your way to Reverend, which is deeply noble. Very few are so charged by God and the saints to take this hard path of their faith. And your faith was clearly tested, especially now."

"My faith is ever strong, sir."

"And remained so, even when the madness of Kellirac sought to affect you. Laudable, Aurien. Very laudable. Which is why I'm happy to tell you, after some deliberation with my priests, we all agree that you have fulfilled the requirements of your Walk."

"Sir?" Pemmick was even more confused.

"And therefore, with the authority vested upon me by his royal majesty and head of the church, King Maradaine XVII, as well as the Archbishop of Acoria, I hereby designate you Reverend of the Church of Druthal."

Pemmick wasn't certain how to react to this. "I

am honored, your grace, to be so worthy, but I still worry that…"

"Of course you worry. You have been through a trial of faith and emerged from the other side. God would not make us capable of questioning if they did not want us to question."

"Thank you," Pemmick said. "If I may, I would like to return to Kellirac, take up the post that Andale held there, see what more I can learn by living with those people."

"Out of the question, Reverend," the Bishop said. "They have killed Andale, and probably nearly killed you. It's best to get you far from here. Back to the heart of civilization, I think, rather than out here on the border near the madness. Yes, the Bishop of Maradaine owes me a favor, I think he could find a place for you." He finished his wine and stood up. "Now you must excuse me. You are at liberty in the cathedral and the citadel, of course, until your formal assignment comes through." He gestured for Pemmick to go to the door.

"Of course, your grace," Pemmick said. "Thank you."

Pemmick went back to his assigned cell. Maradaine. He had never been out there, so far west. He had to admit, he was interested in the potential of that. And he was more than happy to not stay in the High Cathedral of Gorivow any longer than necessary.

He could not reconcile what he saw in Kellirac, what he knew to be true, with what he had been told, but he would not forget it. But even still, he knew, there was a deeper truth than he was being told. Yes, the story the bishop told him could fit the facts, but didn't feel remotely correct to the truth.

And there was quite a lot of silver in this cathedral.

The ring was real. The scar on his wrist where the skeletal hand had scraped him was real. What he saw was real.

Regardless of what he had been told, who was lying and who was honest, he knew what he knew to be true.

Faith would guide him.

ACKNOWLEDGMENTS

This is a story that's been sitting with me, in various forms, for a while, and even when it was finished— at least the relatively final draft— I wasn't sure what to do with it. What was I going to do with these stranger shorter pieces connected to the Maradaine Saga? This past year brought a lot of clarity, and with that clarity, the opportunity to create these "Maradaine Saga Shorts" with Artemisia, letting me put these smaller stories on the fringe of Maradaine into your hands.

That opportunity was shepherded by the work I've been doing on my podcast Worldbuilding for Masochists, and I can't express how much my co-hosts, Rowenna Miller and Cass Morris, are just the best people to work with. Brilliant, creative minds, and incredible anchors of support. I couldn't ask for better partners on the podcast, and I'm blessed to have their friendship, especially in this past year.

Absolutely essential for this book was Britta Jensen, who continues to be a source of insight and inspiration. Very grateful for her counsel, advise, expertise and friendship. Also instrumental were my usual sounding boards: Daniel Fawcett, forever my absolute rock when it comes to every element of this saga; and Miriam Robinson Gould, the best first reader I could ask for. More support came from patrons and fans, like Brian Yost and Ember Randall.

On top of that, my family remains a source of strength and inspiration. This includes my parents Nancy and Lou, and my mother-in-law Kateri. And, of course, my son Nicholas and wife Deidre, who have continued to put up with me during this incredible journey through Maradaine and beyond.

And thank you, dear reader. Because you have this book in your hands, you've stayed with me in this journey, and I'm so thrilled to have you with me.

ABOUT THE AUTHOR

Marshall Ryan Maresca is a fantasy and science-fiction writer, author of the Maradaine Saga: Four braided series set amid the bustling streets and crime-ridden districts of the exotic city called Maradaine, which includes The *Thorn of Dentonhill, A Murder of Mages, The Holver Alley Crew* and *The Way of the Shield*, as well as the dieselpunk fantasy, *The Velocity of Revolution*. He is also the co-host of the Hugo-nominated, Stabby-winning podcast **Worldbuilding for Masochists**, and has been a playwright, an actor, a delivery driver and an amateur chef. He lives in Austin, Texas with his family.

CPSIA information can be obtained
at www.ICGtesting.com
Printed in the USA
BVHW072354180123
656596BV00015B/107